self-portrait abroad

T0161394

other works by jean-philippe toussaint
in english translation

The Bathroom
Monsieur
Camera
Television
Making Love
Running Away

self-portrait abroad
jean-philippe toussaint

translated by john lambert

Dalkey Archive Press
Champaign and London

Originally published in French as *Autoportrait (à l'étranger)*
by Les Éditions de Minuit, 2000
Copyright © 2000 by Les Éditions de Minuit
Translation copyright © 2010 by John Lambert
First English translation, 2010
All rights reserved

Library of Congress Cataloging-in-Publication Data

Toussaint, Jean-Philippe.
[Autoportrait (à l'étranger). English]
Self-portrait abroad : a novel / by Jean-Philippe Toussaint ; translated by John Lambert.
p. cm.
ISBN 978-1-56478-586-2 (pbk. : alk. paper)
1. Toussaint, Jean-Philippe--Travel. 2. Authors, French--20th century--Biography. 3.
French--Foreign countries--History--20th century. I. Lambert, John, 1960- II. Title.
PQ2680.O86Z4628 2011
843'.914--dc22
                    2009051110

Partially funded by the University of Illinois at Urbana-Champaign
and by a grant from the Illinois Arts Council, a state agency

Ouvrage publié avec l'aide du Ministère français chargé de la Culture –
Centre national du livre

This book was published with the support of the French Ministry of Culture –
Centre national du livre

La publication de cet ouvrage a été encouragée par une subvention
accordée par la Communauté française de Belgique

www.dalkeyarchive.com

Cover: design and composition by Danielle Dutton, illustration by Nicholas Motte
Printed on permanent/durable acid-free paper and bound in the United States of America

Every time I travel I feel a very slight feeling of dread at the moment of departure, a dread sometimes shaded with a soft shiver of elation. Because I know that any trip brings with it the possibility of death—or of sex (both highly improbable of course, yet not to be excluded altogether).

tokyo, first impressions

You arrive in Tokyo the way you arrive in Bastia, from the sky. The plane flies in a long arc above the bay and aligns with the runway to touch down. Seen from above, at four thousand feet, there isn't much difference between the Pacific and the Mediterranean.

Chrisitan Pietrantoni, incidentally, a Corsican friend of Madeleine's—I will call Madeleine Madeleine in these pages to help me get my bearings—promptly got in touch with me to arrange a meeting in a Tokyo café and fill me in on what had been happening back in the village. The very day after my arrival, hardly leaving me the time to unpack my bags, he called me up in my hotel room while, dressed in a white shirt and small blue cardigan of the sort worn by retired teachers (a New Year's gift from my parents), I sat on the bed in my socks flipping through a sports magazine and awaiting the imminent arrival of a journalist who was coming to interview me. Seated at a round table right next to me in the room was Mr. Hirotani of the Shueisha Publishing House, who since the beginning of my stay had been alternating with Mrs. Funabiki as companion and confidante, guide and bodyguard, and who I perceived out of the corner of my eye in a perfect suit and tie, his face grave and attentive, busying himself arranging in a vase a bouquet of flowers I'd been given. He was grappling with five purple and white flowers (the Anderlecht colors, I'm not sure if it was intentional), whose position he altered incessantly to compose a harmonious bouquet, regularly starting over again from scratch, changing here the position of one flower, there the position of another, looking more, it seemed to me, like a thug from a film by Godard than a connoisseur of Japanese floral arrangement. And as I continued to observe him discreetly, lazily turning the pages of my magazine while voluptuously crossing and uncrossing my stockinged feet on the bedspread, the telephone rang out in the room. Dropping his flowers on the carpet, Mr. Hirotani dashed to the telephone in a single bound.

Putting his arm over my head he seized the phone on the bedside table and gave a discreet, courteous pull on the cord which had inopportunely got twisted around my neck and shoulder. Strangling me for an instant while trying to get it untangled, he took the cord cautiously in both hands, passed it over my head and answered the telephone with an apologetic look. My head raised, I tried to guess who he could be talking with, someone from hotel reception or the publisher, perhaps the journalist we were waiting for from *Yomiuri Shimbum*. Standing there beside me he listened gravely, mechanically retying the knot of his tie. *Yes*, he said, *yes. It's for you*, he said, handing me the receiver: Christian Pietrantoni.

I made a date with Christian Pietrantoni for two days later and, after a first missed meeting one night in a South American bar in Roppongi, he came to fetch me one morning at the hotel. Taking off our coats we walked side by side in Tokyo under the island sun before stopping at a modern, insipid, and impersonal café. Although it was pastis time we contented ourselves with a green tea, and, while young girls ate at the next tables in a cacophony of chopsticks and Japanese voices, Christian Pietrantoni, sitting across from me, perfectly indifferent to the surrounding atmosphere, filled me in on the latest news from the village. He told me what Nono and Nénette were up to, the Albertinis, the Antomarchis, what do I know. I wondered what source he had for all his information (perhaps he had correspondents in other Asian capitals?). Accompanying me back to the hotel he gave me what was no doubt one key to the mystery when he let on that he had a subscription to *Corse-Matin*. Before saying goodbye we promised to meet up again soon, in Ersa or Tokyo, London or Macinaggio, then shook hands vigorously the way Westerners do in front of hotel entrances.

I had strange experiences with my hands in Japan. I don't know if it was because of the hotel I was staying at, the types of material the building had been constructed from—the fact, for example, that its doorknobs were mostly made of metal and not wood—or whether the cause of all these little irritations had more to do with my wool cardigan (a New Year's gift from my parents) . . . nevertheless, each time I was about to take hold of a doorknob or press an elevator button, I got a shock of static electricity. But enough of personal matters.

hong kong

We'd landed in Hong Kong a few minutes earlier, flying over the city at a ridiculously low altitude, thirty or so feet at most, the immense mass of the Boeing slamming down onto the runway after barely scraping over the rooftops and flying over a last shop-lined street where you could see men in white shirts, cigarettes in their mouths, crossing the road without paying the least attention to the insane spectacle that this gigantic airplane must have presented overhead, or else standing tranquilly on their doorsteps, arms crossed, taking in the fresh air of this bustling Hong Kong street where thousands of multicolored ideograms blinked continuously in the night. Not long beforehand, when the plane was still much higher in the sky and turning slowly in the air to commence its descent, the entire bay of Hong Kong had suddenly appeared through my window in a twinkling of luminous blue and white points, revealing farther off the presence of other urban concentrations, Macao or Kowloon, whose illuminated agglomerations shone out against a background of bluish mountains barely visible as shadowy profiles in the night. Meanwhile, on the surface of the water below us, among the silhouettes of the cruise ships and barges, cargo and container ships, floating casinos and nightclubs where you could dance the salsa or mambo-mambo under dotted strings of lamps, the navigation lights of thousands of solitary junks rocked slowly to and fro, dotting the bay like so many fireflies.

Seated on one of those anonymous plastic seats in an immense hall at Hong Kong International Airport, I looked at the dirty linoleum floor between my legs, thoughtful, my hands joined and my body inclined, a little lost and disoriented (I'd taken off from Osaka some five hours earlier and was headed for Frankfurt where I was due to land in twelve more hours). I didn't know where I was and no longer really knew where I was going. I'd already had a similar feeling of the momentary loss of temporal and spatial landmarks a few days earlier in the plane that had taken me to Japan when, sitting drowsily in my seat, I suddenly became aware looking out the window that it was neither day nor night outside, but simultaneously day and night, and that to the right of the plane I could see the moon, shining in the sky in-line with the wing, as well as the sun, far out in front of us, which for the moment was still just a blurred pink and orange glow similar to the cottony contours of a Rothko, lighting up the horizon of this immense sky divided evenly into day and night, into Europe and Asia. The silent cabin of my sleepy seven-forty-seven was still convinced of its being night, however, as it flew in perfect stillness toward Tokyo to the hushed droning of its motors, my watch showing one o'clock in the morning, the other passengers dozing around me in the feeble light, the small plastic blinds on the windows carefully lowered, to say nothing of my own fatigue after seven or eight hours of flight, my eyes heavy and closing softly, yes, everything seemed to indicate that it was night—apart from one important detail: it was now broad daylight outside.

My watch now showed something like eleven o'clock in the evening, a Japanese time that was no longer relevant anywhere, neither in Berlin where I was headed nor in Hong Kong where I still was. Because I was in Hong Kong, yes, though I might as well have been in a novel. But enough of verisimilitude.

berlin

The Berliners have a reputation for being terse, impatient, dislikeable. When you go into a store, for example, they say that after having wiped your feet you almost have to apologize for wanting to buy something. When you speak German as badly as I do, and with a strong accent (although the question of accents is entirely relative), you are generally treated with very little patience, and if, after audaciously expressing the desire to purchase something you are reckless enough to ask that the person behind the counter repeat her question with a nevertheless perfect little *Wie bitte?*, you get snubbed all the more for having cast suspicion on the way the question had been formed, although it was in perfect German, judge for yourselves: *Wie dick, die Scheibe?* Normal, I said, a normal slice: The young woman, because it was a young woman, a mean and pudgy young woman, looked at me with suspicion. She cut me a slice of ham, threw it down on the counter. *Noch einen Wunsch? Das*, I said, and I pointed at a tray of aspic. She hurriedly cut a minuscule slice of aspic, I mean really minuscule, at best you could have coated your passport with a slice of jelly that thin, or wiped your glasses off. *Dicker*, I said. That was the turning point in our encounter, I said it very dryly, and, immediately, without weakening, I looked her intensely in the eyes with a mean stare, and there were only two possible outcomes, either she would send me packing with an insult, explaining while kicking me out of the shop that as I had not indicated the thickness of the slice she was entitled to assume I'd wanted it very thin (which, if she'd rattled it off in German, I could hardly have contested), or she would buckle and cut my slice as I wanted. She obeyed. Putting the minuscule slice to one side, to eat later, who knows, to roll it into a ball and swallow it in an idle moment, she took the whole dish from the window. She placed the knife on the terrine and gave me an inquisitive look. Like that? she said. Bigger, I said. She moved the knife to the right. Like that? she said. A little bit smaller, I said. She lifted her eyes and gave me a look, but she no

16

longer resisted, now she was under my thumb. Again she moved the knife to the right. No, no, not so big! I said. She moved the knife to the left, quicker and quicker now, things were accelerating more and more, she moved the knife slightly to the left, slightly to the right, slightly to the left, slightly to the right, she couldn't get it right, she was unable to satisfy me. Too bad, you had it, I said. Start from the beginning, I said. She stopped, lifted her knife from the terrine. She was perspiring, large beads of sweat fell into the dish. Relax, I said, you're too overwrought. Come on, give it another try. Like that? she said. Perfect, I said. You see, I said, if you really put your mind to it, and I almost stroked her cheek. She wrapped my slice with care and handed me my change with infinite respect. She was at a loss as to what else she could do for me, what to propose, what favor she could bestow upon me, a plastic bag perhaps, a little aperitif, could she call me a taxi? I left without saying good-bye (I don't like unpleasant people).

prague

Let's not talk about Prague. We spent a lover's weekend there, Madeleine and I, around Easter, in an almost windowless attic room which gave the impression of being in some tawdry flophouse, with its mezzanine floor and half-closed blinds, dark, dusty, a bit smelly (we left an envelope with a couple of deutschemarks on the coffee table for the little racketeer who'd sublet it to us when we left).

And yet the trip had started off well enough. In Berlin, full of hope and using my German, which got better by the hour, I'd reserved two very promising train tickets for Prague in a travel agency on Kurfürstendamm, one of those large and prosperous travel agencies whose bay windows carry an ever-changing array of yellow and white banners with mouthwatering travel suggestions, listing prices and destinations with unbeatable offers for trips to the Balearic Islands, Florida, or Tunisia. I'd bought two train tickets for Prague, two first-class seats on the morning train that passes through Prague once a day on its way to Budapest, one of those old-fashioned trains that makes you drool just looking at it, all decked out with velvet upholstery with small nets for newspapers on the seats, pillow headrests, and lovely velvet footrests as soft as cushions and as round as prayer benches. No sooner had we left—our bodies reclining in our adjustable seats, our shoes already off—than we started to unfold our newspapers and flip through them leisurely, Madeleine and I, softly rubbing our stockinged feet; at first every man for himself in the unreflecting comfort of solitary reading, then, little by little, together, mingling our feet and arms to the unbridled delight of our senses, uniting our mouths in the euphoria of the voyage we were commencing, our legs, our hands, what do I know, our thighs, our hips. You don't know how to make love in a train, she said with a smile.

We'd gone back to the restaurant car and, after a studious browse through the greasy old menus wrapped in wine-colored plastic proposing in Czech and German different types of sausage and pork embellished with an unavoidable side of potatoes, we ordered the most expensive dishes on the menu, pork and sausages, it was either that or fried eggs, asking our waiter to throw in two bottles of cold Czech beer. We'd already drunk a few sips of fresh Budweiser and were calmly eating our meal, now and then giving each other a bit of pork across the table, more like an attentive couple than enflamed and suicidal Bohemian lovers ladling sizzling drops of zabaglione into each others' mouths with long silver spoons (as Madeleine and I used to do when we were young), when, in this almost deserted restaurant car whose touching old-fashioned decorations we found endlessly delightful, the sun suddenly shone through the clouds and lit up the Saxony countryside. That is the image I will remember from this trip, Madeleine and I sitting face to face in the sunny restaurant car on our way to Prague. The winding shores of the Elbe flashed by the compartment window as the train hugged its curves, chugging along beside the river, accompanying its bends and meanders. I'd finished my beer a few moments earlier and my whole being was bathed in the feather-light beginnings of drunkenness, massaging my temples like an aura of honey. Rocked by the imminent

20

promise of Prague (which no reality, however small, had yet tarnished), I looked at Madeleine who smiled across from me in the fullness of our intact hopes while the air shimmered around us, wafting softly and lightly along the stitched lace curtains of the compartment window, above our plates, over the knives and forks, over our glasses, over our hands entwined on the table, over the flies.

cap corse (the best day of my life)

The day had begun in a perfectly innocuous way. We were expecting a couple of friends for lunch on this Wednesday, August 10 (the date is now forever engraved in my memory), and we'd already set the table in the garden in the shadow of a large white canvas parasol. Madeleine was varnishing the wooden shutters while waiting for our friends to arrive, wandering thoughtfully along the front of the house in her bathing suit with a bowl of Fongexor varnish and a paintbrush in her hand, on the lookout for any spots on the shutters in need of a handy touch up here or there (or on the wooden table, the chair legs, the parasol stand—everything was fair game for her when it came to Fongexor, so watch your pricks). As I walked back blithely toward the house after taking a swim among the rocks, my hands in the pockets of my baggy Bermuda shorts, I noticed a little poster tacked to the spotted trunk of a plane tree at the turn coming into the village, a rectangular white poster announcing a boules tournament in perfect type (a font called "New York," if I'm not mistaken). The contest was to take place the same day in the neighboring village of Tollare in the middle of the afternoon, and it just so happened that Ange Leccia, who we were expecting for lunch, was my official boules partner. The fact was that Ange and I were what you might call enlightened enthusiasts. We focused on every point and didn't squander our boules, making calculated and circumspect throws after studying the terrain by digging in our heels to gauge its softness and ductility, and then returning pensively to the circle, crouching down and pointing with equanimity. As a team we were somewhat lacking in practice and method, and in agility as well, we weren't exactly spring chickens, and of course being rather more alike than complementary in style we lacked the panache of a real team, with its natural-born, instinctive shooters (we were both pointers, unfortunately, crouching low to the ground like little old men). In short, and to give an honest summary of our boules season so far, we'd got past the first round at Muro before being eliminated by a couple of tourists, two awkward and lucky freeloaders on vacation, and we'd cancelled our participation at the tournament in B. for personal reasons.

Once we'd finished lunch we lost no time in loading the pétanque balls into the trunk of the 4x4, when what I at first took for a couple of particularly brazen Italian tourists pulled up and parked their Vespa right in front of the terrace, practically where we were standing. Seated on the back of the motorcycle, whose exhaust pipe continued to bang and spit out a nasty-smelling little cloud of black smoke around our legs, sat a Japanese woman dressed in a large white tank top that all but revealed the naked curve of her breasts, a Japanese woman who, not seeming at all ready to dismount, remained seated on the back of the scooter looking every bit like some hitherto unclassified mythological creature (neither siren nor seahorse: the top half a Japanese woman and the bottom half a scooter), carefully holding a bright yellow surfboard under her arm. It was only the rather uncustomary presence of this Japanese woman on the back of the motorcycle that stopped me from immediately recognizing the driver. Getting off with calm assurance he propped the Vespa on its stand

and took off his sunglasses in a Hollywood-like gesture: Christian Pietrantoni. Dressed in a flowery shirt, Bermuda shorts, and long, vaguely Austrian spotted white woolen socks pulled up to his knees (attire that contrasted somewhat with the austere gray suit and small round glasses he'd been wearing the last time I'd seen him in Tokyo), he introduced us to Noriko, who'd just got off the scooter, effectively delaying our departure for the boules tournament. I served them a well-cooled glass of Orenga rosé on the terrace while Christian Pietrantoni spent the entire conversation pulling up his Tyrolean socks and leaning over to his friend to exchange a few loud words with her in Spanish, the only language they both understood, she having spent several years in Madrid (the same years I had, in fact, I learned to my surprise: *¡hombre, en el ano noventa!* said the Japanese woman, *¡Yo tambien!*). Christian Pietrantoni had for his part been posted to London at the time, which probably had no connection with his excellent knowledge of Castilian. Ange knew Christian Pietrantoni too of course, Ange knew everyone. I'd even heard that when Ange's parents came to visit him in Tokyo (Ange had also lived in Japan for a bit: "Really, these Corsicans are everywhere," the Japanese woman must have thought), Christian Pietrantoni, immediately filled-in about their arrival by some well-informed snitch or another (Ange himself probably), had swooped down on their hotel with all the swiftness of a predator and all the doting attention of a Lithuanian cousin to serve as their guide and companion, leading them through the narrow streets of Shinjuku and telling them about the country while bringing himself up to date on the latest news from the village, the most recent *putachji* from Centuri, Morsiglia, or the hamlet of Minerviu. I glanced discretely at the time and, not wanting to be late for the boules match, abruptly signaled our departure by impetuously clacking my pétanque balls together the way the great players do, making Noriko jump in her seat (*¡santo cielo!* she cried, putting a hand to her chest).

We headed off. Taking our seats in the different vehicles we drove over to Tollare in a slow, motorized procession, Christian Pietrantoni's little Vespa leading the way through the silent and burning scrubland, while we boules players followed in Ange's 4x4 without speaking a word, like astronauts with less than an hour before takeoff. In front of us Christian Pietrantoni swerved his

Vespa along the sinuous bends in the road like a motor-cycle escort, swaying back and forth with the curves. Behind him, Noriko was clutching the multicolored shirt of her knight errant in one hand and her yellow surfboard in the other, like some profane trophy she was parading from one village to the next in honor of the ocean and its enormous waves (even if the Mediterranean was calm as a lake that day, with just a few little waves perishing humbly against the rocks down below). When we got to Tollare we parked on the large gravel lot and I walked down to the beach to sign us up for the tournament. In a little shack surrounded by reeds where you could buy ice cream and a few soft drinks, a table had been set up under a parasol and two guys in shorts (the organizers) signed the players in before starting the draw. Reaching my hand deep into the pocket of my Bermuda shorts I took out a crumpled old fifty franc note displaying a wizened, grinning Voltaire, and gave our names to the organizers. They just took down our first names, Ange, Jean-Philippe, Jean-Michel (Vilmouth's first name is not Jean-Michel, by the way, but Jean-Luc, everyone knows that; no matter, later I astutely made up for my slip by telling him I'd invented the pseudonym to help him save face once people had seen him point). When it was finally time for the draw with its unchanging ritual of little scraps of paper mixed together in a cotton sunhat sporting the Pastis 51 emblem, luck had it that my partner was a certain René. Our team was rather unbalanced, I must say, you couldn't have imagined a more disparate, morganatic pair. René, short and stocky, densely muscled, with a thin black moustache, red shorts, and some old slippers (he could even have gone shirtless), was the infallible shooter, while I, long-limbed and aristocratic (very Prince of Savoie, I'd been told), had the fine long hands of a levelheaded pointer, legs looking rather white compared with my partner's hairy brown stumps (though, as far as I was concerned, my legs were already ideally tanned), silhouette slightly hunched by the weight of my years and with a hint of lukewarm disdain about it, thanks to the daily exercise of irony. I was wearing a simple baggy pair of beach trunks and a loose white cotton shirt, a light-colored straw hat that fit me like a glove—an elegant yellow straw boater garnished with a fine caramel ribbon that must have belonged to my grandfather Lanskoronskis—and a pair of what are known as boat shoes, the sort worn by indolent rich amateur sailors who idle away their time on yacht-club gangways (you can imagine the sort of figure I cut: people called me Monsieur). After the first game, which of course we won without difficulty, we returned to the shack to announce our rapid victory to the organizers. The other games were still in progress, only one had already ended, apparently without much of a fight, I could see Jean-Luc (disguised as Jean-Michel, three pétanque boules scattered around his feet) leaning on a white plastic chair on the terrace, his pant legs rolled up around his calves, standing there in bare feet gazing out at the sea. And? I asked him. Thirteen to zero, he said, and lazily tossed a pebble into the water that, like him, succumbed, dropping slowly to the bottom, two arm's lengths from where Noriko was paddling, her surfboard wedged under her arms, slowly advancing over the water, kicking her legs recklessly behind her in the blue, desperately still sea.

Ange and I both made it easily to the semi-finals and I must say that, seeing us fighting out the tournament's two semi-finals just a few meters apart, each with a different partner (who, although not our regular partners, no doubt gave us better odds), it struck me we were heading straight for a fratricidal confrontation in the finals. Things didn't turn out that way (and this isn't the place for me to explain the reasons for Ange's early defeat). When it came to the finals, crouching down in the circle to point, concentrating, my panama on my head, my shoes covered with a fine coating of gravel dust, I noticed that a small crowd had gathered on the main square of the village, and was looking on attentively. My boule in my hand, now completely immersed, my eyes intense, I sized up the distance separating my boule from the jack and gave myself mental pointers like, "Don't throw it too short now" (because I tend to be short—in boules that is). Taking one last look at my target, slightly to the left of the natural axis of the slope, and tracing one last time in my mind the entire trajectory of my boule, I finally straightened in the circle, almost in slow motion, and, in the same all-embracing synchronous movement, I lifted my arm and let go of the boule with a final, minutely calculated rotational twist of the wrist. It was short, damn it, I could see it right away. Point another, go on, said René, violently clacking his two boules together to calm his nerves (and perhaps so as not to take his disappointment out on me in a more physical manner). I crouched back down in the circle. From time to time I recognized a few familiar voices in the vague noise of the crowd. *Yo qué el hubiera saccado*, Noriko was saying. *Cres aue va a apuntar otra vez?* she added. *Callate, lo vas a descentrar*, answered Christian Pietrantoni. Not able to concentrate, in fact, I didn't play right away and got up to have another look at the position of the balls, dropping my boule vertically onto the ground to calculate the resistance of the terrain. Not too short, hmm? said René. No, no, I saw, I saw, I said. I went back to the circle and pointed (I was long, a hair long). At the end of the game, on the last throw, our opponents were leading eleven to nine and the fate of the game hung in the balance. I had the chance to shoot for the win and put all four of our balls closest to the jack. You gotta shoot, said René, you gotta shoot, it's all or nothing. Though I always concentrate for a long time before pointing, I generally shoot by instinct. I went up to the circle and without a moment's reflection shot and . . . knocked their boule from the center. And my boule stayed put. There was a moment of hesitation in the square, murmurs, a buzz of voices, the score was counted. Nine plus four: thirteen. Thirteen, we'd won the competition (the first prize was a Corsican ham, a *prizuttu*). A vague stir started up around me, people came up on all sides to offer their congratulations, my son jumped up and down for joy, Madeleine ran over to me with our baby Anna in her arms, who uttered her first words on the spot in a burst of enthusiasm (either "papa" or "*prizuttu*"; no one was really sure in the confusion). The organizers then awarded me the first prize of the competition, the Corsican ham. Moved, I took it in both hands and brought it to my lips before holding it up at arm's length to the crowd while shots were fired and bells rang out all around the village. I then passed the ham to my partner and he kissed it in turn, rubbing it against his moustache, and, in the general hubbub, with Noriko trotting alongside and holding out her surfboard for me to autograph, we did a little victory march around the village square, followed by a limping dog and a couple of kids.

I dedicate these Corsican pages to my wife and children (and thank my teammate).

tokyo

I don't know the exact name in French, even less what it's called in Japanese. But what constantly, sometimes painfully, and always tellingly marked the first three weeks of my stay in Japan was the *scruchjètta*. Not a simple back pain, not really lumbago, not quite sciatica, the *scruchjètta* (the word is Corsican) is a sort of pain in the kidneys that can strike you at any time, while you're picking up your boules over a game of pétanque (crack and you're stuck, knees stiff, a hand on your back, unable to straighten up), or carrying an outboard motor down a slippery boat launch in a little fishing port on the way to your boat. All things considered I owe my *scruchjètta* to the unhappy concurrence of two causes, one you could call structural, linked to the general weakening of my back since this summer when I carried my daughter down to the beach on my shoulders every day (she's only two but she already puts it away like a little *sumotori*), and the second, more conjunctural, being that as I was trying one day at the end of the summer to put back a shutter I'd repainted with Madeleine, leaning out the first floor window into the emptiness, I made an abrupt turning movement that twisted my spine.

Now if there's one country where it's anything but ideal to have the *scruchjètta*, it's Japan. Even if it's got a surface area of almost one hundred and fifty thousand square miles, that's not the impression you get when you're there. To enter any public space, be it a restaurant in Gion or a dark little café in the narrow streets of Shinjuku, a tiny basket or lacquer shop whose smallness is apparent as soon as you walk in the door, you have to bend over on entering and walk with your head down while contorting yourself around the shelves, all the time making sure you don't bang your head against a kakemono or knock over an entire shelf of precious ceramics, tea pots, or little saké glasses with your backpack while turning around. No sooner had I reached the end of a corridor, the other day, at a restaurant, wearing a vague stoic grimace, than I had to take off my shoes. Now if this operation is relatively easy, ordinarily, and hardly requires the limberness of a grasshopper, things are entirely different when you have a *scruchjètta*, because every time you bend down toward the ground, no matter how minutely, no matter how gradually, to undo your shoelaces, you're hit with an often searing pain. But I managed it. After taking off my shoes then and there with the precaution of a diplomat, I entered a silent hall, the wool of my socks swishing softly against the tatami, and then, cautiously, a magnificent traditional dining room with thin movable partitions made of translucent white paper. I crossed the room silently on tiptoes and sat down on one of the cardinal red (or purple or fuchsia, a ceremonial color) *zabuton*s arranged around a low black lacquer table. Sitting immobile in the room like a foreign dignitary, cross-legged, or in the lotus position, or first one then the other, I kept changing my posture as the courses came and went in front of me, kneeling, looking straight ahead, my legs forming first a *Y*, then an *L*, a *P*, an *R*, an &, and finally, a complete wreck, a poor M with two branches, a pitiful hiragana, a defeated katakana.

As, apart from a few courses in calligraphy, I'd intended to take cooking lessons during this trip to Japan to learn how to cut fish properly, according to the rules of this art, Mr. Sudo of the Shueisha Publishing House, who fulfilled my every wish as soon as I expressed it and sometimes before I even managed to spit it out, took me with him one night to his local sushi restaurant. There, in this little traditional sushi bar with light wood interiors just a stone's throw from his office, Mr. Sudo was at home. It was his restaurant, his family, his clique, his canteen. He must have filled the owner in on the somewhat unusual though by no means ignominious nature of my desires because no sooner had we entered than I found myself clad in a white apron that was quite difficult to get into (you had to put it on a bit like a parachute, first attaching the lateral straps then passing the whole thing over your head), and brought through a serving door into an extremely cramped kitchen, overcrowded with shelves and cupboards. There, after being guided through the utensils, I was asked to be good enough to wash my hands in a little floor-level washbasin, perfect for washing your feet, and, crouching down on the ground, I rinsed my hands in the running water before my host, who'd been looking on very kindly, showed me how to work the little inverted cylinder holding a syrupy greenish liquid soap. Having soaped my hands I straightened up and, coming over to the sink while giving my hands a quick wipe on my apron, I discovered two identical fish waiting for us on the counter, two small pink and shiny sea bream. I took my place beside the cook and attentively watched him work. He set about carefully scaling the bream with a large hatchet-shaped knife, holding the blade very high, very straight (I would have proceeded a bit differently, but that was perhaps just a question of style, the way two ping-pong players can have entirely different but equally irreproachable ways of holding their rackets). Then he cut off its head with a deliberate oblique thrust, from the top of the head to the bottom of the upper ventral fin. Working away with the knife he then gutted the fish with a series of delicate slashes and scrapes. He rinsed his knife under the tap. Now it's your turn, he made me understand by threatening me amiably with the knife. I took the bream by the head and laid it smoothly on the cutting board. My knife sank into its flesh and I went about scaling it. As I progressed I could see the owner beside me, watching me work with a sorry sort of look, kindly shaking his head all the while to signify "no," concerned and sympathetic, "no, not a chance." When I'd finished I bent under the sink to throw out the viscous fish guts in a large garbage bag and straightened up, with sticky fingers and a slight grimace, one hand on the tender part of my back afflicted with the *scruchjètta*, and washed my hands under the tap. Several fish came and went in this way in front of us on the workbench, breech, sardines, plaice, flounder, which we gutted and cut into pieces while my host rounded out my cook's training the whole time with detailed explanations in Japanese. At one moment, adding even more to the confusion, or in an effort to reduce it, the small curtain separating the kitchen from the restaurant opened and Mr. Hasegawa popped his head inside, the editor of a review called *Subaru*. A minuscule dictionary in his hand, he started translating the cook's explanations into English, indicating as he went along the French names of the fish we were busy cutting up. This is a mackerel, he said. I'd have said it's a bonito, I said. A mackerel, a mackerel, he repeated, nodding his head rapidly in confirmation (in Japanese you generally avoid contradicting the person you're talking with too directly, and never say for example, "*no*, it is not a bonito," but—when the context allows, that is—"*yes*, it's a mackerel"). A big mackerel, then, I said. A big mackerel, he conceded, sinking his eyes into his little dictionary, which he went back to flipping through feverishly in the doorway. When I'd finally finished preparing my mackerel filets and was somewhat sheepishly arranging the fragmented hunks of flesh on the wooden cutting board with the tip of my knife to make four more or less respectable filets, the cook, standing there beside me in perplexity, leaned over the shapeless mass of hacked mackerel and explained to me with much respect—Mr. Hasegawa was translating—that considering their pitiful condition they were unfit for sashimi, and asked how I'd like them cooked, should they be grilled, fried? Grilled, grilled, I said (raw fish is also good grilled).

kyoto

I didn't get much chance to improve my German in Kyoto. A few weeks after I arrived I had a visit from my friend Romano Tomasini, a violinist with the Berlin Philharmonic Orchestra (of Italian origin, Romano is actually from Luxembourg, but we generally speak French when we're together). After visiting a few temples Romano proposed we drop in on an acquaintance of his (a German painter married to a Japanese woman, who'd settled in Japan thirty or so years ago) whom he'd met a few years earlier in a lounge at an international airport, their two flights being late, or his only, no matter. Romano had called his friend that morning, who had suggested we pass by his place that afternoon. Equipped with an address written in kanji on a visiting card, we hailed a taxi and got in, showing the visiting card of this

Hans-Joachim von R. to the white-gloved driver at the wheel with whom we spoke for a moment (in Japanese, then in English—Romano tried German and Italian but didn't bother with Luxembourgish) before getting back out: the driver couldn't quite see what we were getting at. I then suggested that Romano call his friend to ask for more detailed information about his address and, having done so, now armed with an incontestable open sesame (the name of a temple), we caught another taxi whose driver set the meter and started off without a moment's hesitation.

We drove along for about an hour in Kyoto, then left the metropolitan area and started toward the mountains that surround the city, heading off along the hillside, the meter now indicating over six thousand yen. Finally the taxi stopped in front of what looked like an abandoned carpentry workshop with a large open shed alongside a pathway. Long narrow strips of rough wood prickly with shavings were fixed to workbenches inside, and a carpet of sawdust as fine as autumn moss covered the ground. The driver turned around to say something that, despite my modest trilingualism and Romano's diverse linguistic talents, we couldn't understand. Romano nodded his head affirmatively and once more showed him Hans-Joachim von R.'s finely embossed visiting card over the seat. The driver examined the visiting card attentively and finally got out of the taxi. He wandered along the street for a few moments before asking a woman for directions, after which he got back into the car with a skeptical look, did a U-turn and drove slowly along the side of the road for a few minutes more before pulling up onto the sidewalk and turning off the motor. There, the visiting card in his hand, he picked up the car telephone and dialed Hans-Joachim von R.'s number. It rang once, twice, then connected, and we heard Hans-Joachim von R.'s distant voice saying in German something like: "We're not in right now, but you can leave a message after the beep." Beeep.

We'd left the cab and had been walking for some time along a deserted road when, coming up to an abandoned intersection, we were witness to a radically bizarre and silent scene. In the middle of the street, down on the asphalt, there was a racing cyclist in a pair of tight-fitting black cycling shorts and a shiny pink polyester jersey with a blue and white pattern. Beside him on the ground was a twisted racing bike, and beside that a car had come to a stop at right angles to the traffic, a perfectly normal car of which all we could see was a bit of the front end, slightly damaged, one broken light bearing solitary witness to the accident. There was no other damage, nothing but a small heap of tiny glass fragments lying on the road. The most astonishing thing about the scene was the absolute still-ness of the central figure, the cyclist, not lying on the road but sitting in despair in the middle of the intersection like a tableau vivant, his two hands on his neck, like an apoc-ryphal image of the sufferings of Christ. More or less at the same time, getting louder in the silence, the echoes of an ambulance siren could be heard far off, which, by I know not what perfect spatiotemporal coincidence, pulled up and parked right in front of me the moment I was about to cross the road, even blocking my view of Romano for an instant, who, in a manner less Nipponese than Neapolitan, had rushed over and knelt down beside the injured cyclist to find out how he was. I could see him talking in a low voice (in Italian?), one hand on the cyclist's shoulder, softly stroking his head to comfort him, while a bit further off a uniformed policeman stuffed the twisted racing bike into a large transparent plastic bag with the help of a gloved assistant. I walked around the ambulance while the stretcher bearers, after asking the few onlookers to make room, carefully lifted the cyclist, still mummified in his sitting position, set him on a stretcher and carried him off precariously balanced like a figurine in a Holy Week procession, before loading him into the back of the ambulance. Romano crossed the street once more amid the glass debris and posted himself at the angle of the intersection, where I saw him suddenly lift his thumb to hitch-hike as the next car drove by. I don't know if it was because of the red light or the ambulance (in any case you're guaranteed success if you hitch-hike in front of an ambulance), nevertheless the car screeched to a halt in front of him and I saw Romano lean in the window and talk to the driver, holding Hans-Joachim von R.'s finely embossed little visiting card in his hand. After a moment he opened the rear door and turned toward me, beckoning for me to come over. I trotted across the road and got into the car, sliding over the back seat as far as an empty baby seat would let me, and nodded politely to the young couple up front. The car started off and we raced after the ambulance, escorted by two police motorcyclists who cleared the way. Sitting in the back of the car I didn't say a thing, somewhat embarrassed to impose on the kindness of this couple and to use Japanese public funds to get an escort to the house of this Hans-Joachim von R. (who wasn't at home, it turned out).

nara, historic capital of japan

Sitting with Professor H. in one corner of the covered café terrace opposite the main entrance to the Nara train station, we kept our eyes peeled for the three people we were supposed to meet. Like a couple of cops on a stakeout, in front of the large window, an old *Japan Times* spread casually out in front of us, we turned our spoons slowly in our cups while casually glancing down the esplanade which bustled with hundreds of people, trying to pick out Charlie or Rémi in the crowd, while I vaguely tried to picture the young woman Professor H. wanted to introduce me to (an admirer, he'd told me, which augured well).

A passionate Francophile and skillful go-between, Professor H. had planned to get the five of us together that day at Nara to take in the city's traditional holiday, *On matsuri*, the last preparations for which were just underway: a couple of guys in *fundoshi* and long blue socks bearing the colors of their brotherhood scuttled across the esplanade with wooden rams in their hands to catch up with a procession that had just departed. Our quintet finally assembled, we hastily introduced ourselves to one another under a driving rain and left the station to go take up a position at the top of a sloped street where we waited for the procession to arrive, Rémi and Professor H. under a huge black umbrella, Charlie and my admirer squeezed together under a smaller transparent one, and myself a little to one side, my hands in my pockets, head down, my black wool hat pulled over my ears. Soon the first horsemen appeared, followed by a long silent procession bearing immense warlike standards that twirled in the wind and sagged under the rain. Unfathomable samurai in damascened armor filed slowly by, followed by hundreds of extras dressed in sumptuous costumes, pleated blue and lilac silks that the rain pressed against their bodies. Soaked and heavy, the tissue finally shed its colors bit by bit, which trickled down into the gutters in blue and white rivulets. Immobile, my collar pulled up around my neck, a few raindrops dribbling down my nose and cheeks, I watched the last breathless figures walking up the street in their soaking sandals, bent double under a torrential rain which became stronger and stronger, a thick, heavy, driving rain like a mobile wall of water that the wind spun in whirls under the stormy black sky; children of around three or four with swords at their belts whose mothers trotted along beside them, all tangled up in their drenched kimonos, trying to cover them with umbrellas blown inside-out in the gusts of wind; stoic, impassive old men on horseback with hundred-year-old stable-boys clutching the reins in both hands, when suddenly the animal bucked in the street in an effort to free itself, whinnying up at the storm, shrieking its rage at the inclement skies (too bad it's raining, huh? I said, leaning over to Professor H.).

After lunch, coming back into the center of town under the persistent rain, I'd let myself fall back and was walking along dreamily beside my admirer. She'd prepared a whole list of questions for me, on my work and my methods, my tastes and how I spent my leisure time, and I felt more like I was giving an interview than engaging in tranquil conversation with a young woman after lunch. To this rather unpleasant impression of being grilled while still digesting my food was added the fact that my admirer remained icily cold in the face of my attempts to break up her interminable seriousness with a bit of humor (she didn't laugh and never smiled), and, as I spoke, I had to face the obvious: she didn't understand French, or just a little (and above all she pronounced it very badly, I had to strain enormously to understand even a word of what she was saying: she pronounced, for example, a word like "fear" as though it were "weeuhh!," which caused me to raise a perplexed eyebrow while continuing to wonder what answer I might possibly give her). To attenuate the disagreeable picture these remarks might give of my admirer, I must admit she got things off to a very good start by telling me that my books had the same beneficial effect on her as Chinese medicine, in that, while never resorting to direct or invasive procedures, nevertheless brought her a strange sense of well-being. I'd been enchanted by this metaphor (a Chinese doctor, that's what I was at heart), and I walked along beside her with an impetuous stride, my shoes light and carefree, avoiding with rollicking dexterity the numerous deer droppings scattered here and there in strands along the ground (you've got to watch out, Nara is full of deer), when I noticed, as we walked, that she was staring at me.

I even had a fleeting feeling at the time that she was going to declare her love for me. You know, you're not at all the way I imagined when I read your books, she avowed in a hushed voice. (What did I tell you?) Oh no? I asked, full of curiosity, suavely stroking a deer under its neck. No, no, she said, in fact I imagined you more small, more intelligent and more blue. More small and more blue! I said, digging in to the deer's fur and twisting it discretely in my fingers to hide my nervousness. (Certain great successes can be founded on immense misunderstandings.) No, no, whiter, she meant more white (more pale, let's say). I had heard wrong (she pronounced *blanc* like *bleu*, which of course might lead to some confusion). We started walking again, I took a disgruntled little kick at an old newspaper lying on the ground. You imagined me more intelligent? I asked in a conversational tone. Yes, she said. We kept walking along side by side. I turned and gave her a fixed look (no, she really didn't speak very good French). We could go stroll ourselves along the river, she said (oh yes, why not, I said, if you like). Stroll ourselves along the river!

When we returned, Professor H., having examined the sky and foretold more rain, proposed that rather than spending the afternoon viewing traditional Japanese art or visiting the Shin Yakushi-ji Temple or the Kasuga Taisha Shrine (we'd already seen Todai-ji that morning), we could take in a more popular although in his view equally instructive spectacle: the striptease. From that moment on he decided to do his best to get rid of the only young woman in our midst, my admirer, judging it better not to involve her in this venture because, even if he was willing to have us, his foreign guests, slum it with him (we were obviously his cover-story), he still retained some sense of decorum, gallant enough to wait until after the young woman's departure, even hurrying it along somewhat, before leading us down his favorite dark alleyways. You have to go back to Kyoto now, Yoshiko, he said, looking at his watch with hypocritical concern. I'll go with you if you like, said Charlie (strippers aren't exactly my thing, he said, and they walked off arm in arm toward the station). The last little setback Professor H. had to deal with before satisfying his unavowable desires in Rémi's and my name was our desire to do a bit of Christmas shopping beforehand. Then, our shopping done, just when he must have thought he'd almost reached his goal, we said we wanted to make a last detour to a shop we'd heard sold authentic handmade paper lanterns. Only then, having each acquired one of these expensive lanterns, our arms loaded with two large paper bags full of Christmas presents for our wives and children, costumes and brushes for our daughters, sandals and incense, trinkets and lacquers, we arrived at the entrance to the strip club. Having bought our tickets, we penetrated into the dubious dark of an old theatre smelling of urine and fermented soy and followed a corridor covered with obscene kanji and scrawled katakana where, here and there in the shadows, banged-up and abandoned vending machines displayed cans of Kirin and Sapporo beer. Professor H. couldn't be restrained, and deserted us as soon as we got into the theatre. Professor, Professor! we yelled, reaching out to hold him back, but it was too late, he was gone. Rémi and I, clenching our bags full of Christmas presents, ventured into the dark labyrinth of corridors before going into the filthy bathrooms reeking equally of piss and miso, of shit and soup, the walls tacked with not particularly well-built Asian pin-ups astride huge Japanese motorbikes. Having stoically taken a piss, our noses pressed up against the exhaust pipes of these humongous bikes and doing our best not to breathe (nice place, by the looks of it), we too finally made our way into the striptease hall where, bathed in a shadowy reddish light, a stripper was just finishing her number on a stage surrounded by mirrors and curtains and lit up indirectly by the phallic beam of a dim red spot. We crossed the hall noiselessly and went over to join Professor H., who tilted his head over to us without taking his eyes off the stage and whispered to us to sit down on two seats that had remained free beside him. We set our bags of Christmas presents down beside us in the darkness, arranging them neatly on both sides of our chairs before looking up at the stage where a stark-naked stripper was spreading her legs on the floor and stuffing a little red ping-pong ball into her vagina before making it pop like a champagne cork, pop, which then fell softly back onto her stomach, whereupon she immediately stuffed it back inside her and started this intimate cup and ball game all over again. After these gymnastics, which only did credit to the suppleness of her anatomy (no matter how you looked at it, she was good at what she did, and we gave her a short round of mental applause), she came over to the edge of the stage and spread her legs wide right under the noses of the spectators in the front row, offering them little transparent plastic towels so they could wipe their fingers in case they were overcome by the urge to thrust them into her pussy and rummage around at their leisure for a while. That afternoon in the theatre it was an exceedingly eclectic group who took her up on this offer and started mucking around inside of her—there were young men and old, two well-dressed, elegant businessmen, three or four mean-looking yakuza with faces like syphilitic thugs who gave her a concentrated, attentive feel, and a pale and sickly fellow in a baseball cap and one of those white gauze masks meant to protect you from germs. Then as the stripper continued to look out benevolently at the audience with her legs spread at the edge of the stage, never losing her perpetual friendly smile like that of an Asian-American television hostess nor seeming to be at all aware that three guys were kneading her breasts and fingering her pussy with all the diligence of indiscriminate, narrow-minded, monotonous adolescents, she absently wiped the tips of their fingers again and moved slightly to one side to give the next spectators a glimpse of the depths of her soul, taking with her as she went the little pile of used transparent towels which seemed to me the most repugnant thing about this well-oiled ritual. Well, merry Christmas.

vietnam

Francophonie is on the decline in Vietnam, as I ascertained on a ten-day study trip to Hanoi. Just off the plane on the evening of my arrival, my flexible black travel bag in my hand and a bead of sweat on my forehead—stoic, immobile, looking around for my hosts in the jostling nocturnal bustle of the arrival gate, I was accosted by an eager and amiable Vietnamese man. *Möchten Sie ein Taxi?* he asked me. *Nein, danke*, I said to him in my German, which was getting worse with every passing day. *Um nach Hanoi zu fahren*, he added, inviting me to follow him. *Nein, ich danke Ihnen*, I said. I didn't need a taxi (in principle I was being picked up by someone from the French embassy). I got up on tiptoes and looked around once more for my host. Nothing. *Es ist nicht teuer*, the taxi driver insisted, *fünfundzwanzig Dollar. Aber ich brauche kein Taxi*, I said. *Woher sind Sie in Deutschland?* he asked. *Und Sie?* I answered. He looked at me. (It seemed he wasn't German either.)

People in Hanoi tend to get around by motorcycle. The very first time I myself got on one was also in Hanoi, behind Solange. Solange, who'd come to pick me up at the hotel to take me on a tour of the city, had proposed I get on the back of her little Honda, and I'd swung one leg in the air and over the seat with my accustomed ease, a bit like the way I'd heard you straddle a pony (although I'm not much of a horseman either), and once in the seat, not terrifically reassured, I'd propped my two feet on the footrests. Then, as she abruptly pulled away and veered resolutely into the traffic, I completely lost my balance and, not knowing what to do with my hands, after a quick look around, my goodness, I put them on Solange's hips. Actually, I found that very pleasant, driving around Hanoi holding Solange by the waist and talking in her ear in a low voice, feeling the very light fabric of her dress under my fingers. I later found out, however, that it was not exactly done to hold your driver by the waist like that when you were not at all on familiar terms, nor was it proper to close your eyes and rest your head in a melancholy way on her shoulder (mentally humming some Italian serenade), and that in fact there was a handle to grab onto on the back of the bike. Behind Professor Bich, moreover—a professor of comparative literature who was kind enough to take me to visit a historic village just outside Hanoi the following weekend—already better-acquainted with motorcycle etiquette, I didn't have the slightest urge, not even the hint of a temptation, to hold him by the waist. Nguyet, for her part (what an urbane life I lived in Hanoi: Solange, Nguyet, Professor Bich; and that's only to name the ones who shared the favor of their motorcycles with me for a few moments), who was no taller than four foot eleven and weighed eighty-eight pounds at the maximum, had no end of difficulty transporting me—at twice her weight—on her own motorcycle. At first she suggested I drive (don't even think about it! I said, looking at the contraption), then, as she could tell that I was hardly about to give in on this point, we finally set out, she kicked the motorcycle off its stand and pushed it onto the street. Our departure was hesitant, laborious even, we both ran along beside the motorcycle to get it up to speed like a bobsled before jumping onto the seat and zigzagging for fifty or sixty feet down Tran Nhan Tong Street. Finally we got stabilized, Nguyet in front, very serious, sitting perfectly straight on the seat and gripping the handlebars with both hands. Then, as we slowed down to approach an intersection, leaning dangerously to one side or the other as we lost speed, Nguyet tried to keep the motorcycle straight while I, immobile behind her, said to myself, "We're going to fall, we're going to fall" (what a mistake, what a mistake to have accepted this invitation to Vietnam). I was preparing to jump clear when I heard the terrifying honk of a truck just a few feet away, however after a final sinuous, ellipsoid loop we elegantly avoided the impending danger, picked up speed and weaved our way once more into traffic.

In Hanoi, the traffic punctuates each hour of the day and almost every hour of the night. The noise of car horns never stops in the streets, it forms a permanent background noise like an uninterrupted murmur that you could almost forget if it didn't keep coming back at you, it being precisely the function of horns to attract attention, to signal and warn, to drown each other out, outhonk one another. Thousands of horns blow without a moment's silence on the streets, shrill and loud, sharp and repetitive, insistent, some quick and piercing, fired off nearby in short impatient salvoes, others remote, lost, muted by their distance, mainly from mopeds and motorcycles, but also from cars and taxis, tarpaulined trucks and three-wheeled vehicles, buses and vans and sometimes even—lost in the middle of an intersection, hardly audible in the surrounding turmoil—the delicate and isolated tinkle of a bicycle bell.

The traffic in Hanoi is like life itself, generous, inexhaustible, dynamic, in permanent motion, constant imbalance, and slipping into its midst and becoming one with the chaos gives you an intense feeling of being alive. Very often, seated in the back of a cycle rickshaw, I let myself be carried along the streets of Hanoi for hours at a time, abandoning myself to the random succession of crossroads and avenues. I was in the very heart of the traffic, sitting on a moving seat, my arms on the armrests, my feet resting on the small curved grid of the rickshaw seat, with no external protection and within arm's reach of the other bicycles, of the honking motorcycles, of the cars, trucks, and buses passing us, of women stranded in the middle of the traffic, lost, hesitant, a straw hat on their heads and a large flexible bamboo pole resting on their shoulders, eyes darting around, looking for an opportunity to cross the street. I glided over the roads, my feet gently brushing the asphalt, letting myself be pulled along by the traffic and the flow of time, I accepted the movement of life and accompanied it without resistance, my thoughts themselves eventually melting into the flow of traffic. Sometimes I took off one of my shoes and crossed my legs in the basket of the rickshaw, leaning my head back and letting it lie motionless on the seat, my sunglasses weightless on my cheeks. Everything was fluid around me, everything flowed listlessly in the surrounding warmth, time and the traffic, life and the hours of the day, my loves and youth itself, I made no effort to hold time back, I consented to get older, accepted the idea of death with serenity. Time passed and I couldn't do a thing about it, I was pulled along in the flood of Hanoi traffic, and all of that intense stream of traffic flowed along with me in the streets like water in a torrential riverbed, never meeting any obstacles, always avoiding them, sweeping around them and continuing on its way, ever curving, always finding new directions and advancing without resisting or forcing anything, imposing on nothing and nevertheless irresistible, imperious, with the force of the wind, the necessity of the tides.

The day after our arrival in Hanoi our delegation was received at the Writers' Union for an informal meeting with our Vietnamese colleagues (we were a bit like the three musketeers, the four of us who'd come from Paris to speak at this cultural event). We'd taken our places in a large impersonal meeting room on the first floor of a modern building with an archway and balcony, it could have been in East Berlin ten years ago if it hadn't been for the heat, which was, believe it or not, even more oriental and overbearing than it was in Berlin, with Formica furniture and tulle curtains in the large windows, a gray carpet, microphones on the tables (and perhaps in the walls as well), three or four bouquets of flowers placed here and there, and a small rostrum, a simple conductor's stand with a vase and a microphone for the speaker. On the wall behind it, in large plastic letters stuck to the wall, was written a welcome message surrounded by a bouquet of accents: *Gap go nha van viet nam va cac nha van phap*. 3.10.1995. Okay, fine. I'd taken a seat in the middle of one of the arms of the large U that made up the immense working table of the conference hall, on the French side of course, between Olivier Rolin and Tahar Ben Jelloun, and across from us at the other leg sat a row of Vietnamese writers in grayish short-sleeved shirts, grave and impenetrable, who stared at us from behind huge spectacles. Vietnamese writers are generally classified by generation, and we had four generations of Vietnamese writers there in front of us, from the oldest who'd seen the French colonization to the youngest who'd fought against the Americans. Right across from me, pale, bald, and fragile, was a writer of the first generation; another, beside him, of the second generation, almost blind, was squinting straight at me. At the end of the arm of the U, at the glove, let's say, sat the French ambassador, impassive, placidly sucking on a cough drop. Then came the rest of us, the participants, almost all of us were there, three out of four (the fourth was still sleeping at the hotel), calm and serious, somewhat perplexed, with faces and eyes alert—a bit too alert, in fact. Once we'd all sat down around the large U-shaped table our host, the General Secretary of the Writers' Union, went and stood at the rostrum accompanied by a small and trembling interpreter in a short-sleeved grayish shirt who translated his words nervously as he spoke. Once he had finished it was time for a representative from the ministry to take the floor who, getting up and heading over to the rostrum, started to read a very long and very official speech on literature and national character, at least six pages which he read right to the end despite occasional breakdowns in the sound system, which started to crackle and then screech. After ten or so minutes no one was listening anymore to what he was saying, and several little bits of paper traveled discreetly up and down the table, from the cultural counselor to the head of the book office or from the head of the book office to the cultural attaché, which we had to hand along to the person next to us as they passed, whereupon the lucky recipient casually opened the little note between his fingers and read it pensively, thumbs pointed outwards and eyes unfocused, while pretending to be listening attentively to the speaker. At one point, as the speech wore on and on, we saw the door of the conference hall open quietly and two young women appear in the room, distractingly silent and discreet, who with a furtive swishing of their silk tunics started to clear away the teacups we'd been given on our arrival, replacing them with cans of soft drinks and Tiger, the Singaporean beer (although it was just after nine in the morning), before bringing us soup bowls, salads, and spring rolls, cold meats, rice, and raw vegetables. There were several courses which I helped set in front of us on the table, plates of cold pork and small dishes of pâté, toast, and ravioli, as well as small vodka glasses in which they started to pour whiskey, or cognac, depending on which bottle they happened to be holding, so that we could toast later on to friendship and literature (there was something vaguely Lithuanian about all this, not to say frankly pleasant). Soon our hosts casually started opening bottles of beer and pouring them discreetly into their glasses while keeping one eye on the stand where the ministry representative was now explaining that autumn, in Vietnam, was the season of poetry and revolution (oh, the timing couldn't be better, what a good thing we'd come in autumn), and I brought the bowl of soup to my lips to take a sip, blowing cautiously on the surface of the piping-hot liquid. The ministry representative finished his speech to a salvo of applause and the floor was handed over to the French ambassador. Very tall and with wavy black hair, the French ambassador got up and went over to the rostrum, sized us all up, and plunged straight into his speech, a blend of Racine and grunge, with large hands and burning eyes, his voice hoarse and raspy as if it had been scratched by his eucalyptus candy, all of which gave his speech—which was otherwise perfectly suited to the occasion—an extravagant Gaullian touch marked by occasional peaks of enthusiasm paying tribute to the radiant influence of the French presence in Asia (perhaps *radiating* would be a better word, I thought, what with the renewed French nuclear tests in the Pacific). Our Vietnamese hosts listened solemnly, nodding their heads in approval, and even jotted down a few notes now and then (writing sagely in their notebooks, "not only economic, but also cultural radiance" and underlining "cultural"). I didn't know if I was dreaming, at the time, or hallucinating, if she was there with one of our group or just by chance, but in that very conference room where our studious gathering of writers and diplomats had convened for a morning's work, separated from us by only a few Vietnamese colleagues, translators, and linguists, there, I swear, I saw Jane Birkin too.

Then, when it was time to leave, just before noon when almost everything had been eaten (the discussions had continued more informally, with everyone remaining seated and pecking at this or that with their chopsticks, a few spring rolls or a bit of cold meat, using the portable microphone if they had anything to add), the General Secretary of the Writers' Union got up to take stock of our working group, welcoming at the same time the actress and singer Jane Birkin. He approached her shyly and asked her, she being a singer and all, to do us the honor of bringing our session to a close with a little song. Jane Birkin, somewhat embarrassed, kindly declined his offer, not able to dissimulate a wisp of a smile. Something from your repertoire, the General Secretary of the Writers' Union asked her, holding out the microphone. No, no, really, repeated Jane Birkin, who continued laughing and smiling. Our other hosts joined in and started pressing Jane Birkin to sing a song. I don't know exactly how it started, but soon everyone was pleading Jane Birkin to sing, four generations of Vietnamese writers, those who'd fought against the French, those who'd fought the Americans, everyone in the big meeting room was clapping their hands and chanting: a song! a song! We too, the French speakers, started chanting as well out of courtesy to our hosts, together with the people from the French embassy, the university professors, a few translators, and even the French ambassador, despite his sore throat. A song! a song! we all chanted around the large U-shaped conference table. Jane Birkin was laughing and laughing (and she's got a very charming way of laughing and laughing, Jane Birkin). A song! a song! we kept chanting. Jane Birkin couldn't refuse any longer, you can't resist four generations of Vietnamese writers. Finally she got up and, walking briskly along the rows of chairs while pushing back a strand of hair, she took the microphone and started to sing, looking at the ministry representative:

> *Et quand tu as plongé dans la lagune*
> *Nous étions tous deux tout nus . . .*

tunisia

I no longer know exactly how this strange premonition came about, but I was certain I was going to die on this trip to Tunisia. I've often taken the plane in recent years, but ordinarily, apart from a slight apprehension at the moment of departure, which makes itself felt by a vague pressure around the chest and a relaxation of the sphincter, giving me a sudden, if generally unwarranted, desire to take a shit the moment I call the taxi, I leave my apartment without any particular fears, even experiencing the tempered enthusiasm of a seasoned traveler as I enter the airport. To tell the story of this curious premonition from the beginning, however: Everything started, I think, one morning in Berlin, where I was living at the time, when Gilles M. of the French embassy called me up to fill me in on the schedule of my visit to

Tunisia, telling me that, whereas I thought I'd be staying the entire couple of days in Tunis, I would in fact have to give a talk at the French Institute in Sfax, and asking me if I'd rather go there by car or by plane. Although the question might seem perfectly innocent, I must say that the mention of this trip to Sfax secretly had the most devastating effect on me you could imagine, because I was at once absolutely certain that it was there I would die, in the aforementioned Sfax, and that I was being asked to choose my death, as simple as that, by car or by plane, and instead of backing out by evasively citing some last-minute obstacle that prevented me from going on this trip, I demonstrated an extraordinary sangfroid by asking in an admirably neutral voice how long it takes to drive from Tunis to Sfax. Around three hours, he said. Well, do what you think is best, I said in a flat voice (when I hung up, as far as I was concerned, I was already dead).

The trip out to Tunis went without a hitch, and I was given a very cordial welcome. As nothing was planned for the day of my arrival, my host arranged to have me driven around Tunis and the surrounding area. We stopped for a moment in Carthage where there wasn't much to see, just a sign beside a lagoon showing where the ancient Punic harbor had been (I can still see myself sitting in that car by the side of the road, the engine running, rolling down the window to take a quick look at the nonexistent ruins). After a day of historical and literary tourism with its Flaubertian and Shakespearean touch (it was a little like Elsinore in Denmark, where there's also nothing to see), I spent a calm night before my departure for Sfax. We'd finally agreed I would travel to Sfax by car and return to Tunis by plane, so the die had not yet been cast as to the exact circumstances of my demise. The driver from the French Institute who came to pick me up at the hotel early the next morning was a small, courteous and taciturn Tunisian who helped me put my bag in the trunk of the car before we headed off slowly toward Sfax, leaving the suburbs of Tunis behind us in the haze. Sitting beside him with my seat belt fastened I daydreamed while looking out at the countryside and, aided by the heat, I even got a hard-on in the car (a small, inept erection, really, in this official car belonging to the French Institute), peacefully following the flow of my thoughts before dozing off on my seat, ithyphallic and contented. I don't know if I conked out completely, but when I opened my eyes again I saw that we'd entered Sousse.

Good day Madam, I said, sitting up in confusion, good day Madam. It was two women, two archaeologists, one thirty-five and the other sixty, I'm making them a bit younger to be on the safe side, whose car had broken down on their way to Sfax the previous day and who, after having spent the night in Sousse, were looking for a way to drive to Sfax with their equipment and get back to their excavation, an archaeological dig situated around thirty miles south of Sfax, I'd say (I say south but I could just as well say north). Having heard through I don't know what Arab grapevine that a speaker (that's what they call us writers in embassy jargon) was traveling by car from Tunis to Sfax, and no doubt unaware of the fateful premonitions of said speaker, they'd asked if the driver of the French Institute's car could take a detour through Sousse and pick them up with their gear, a complete set of six or seven suitcases full of mysterious archaeological material, big padded honeycombed metal suitcases like they use in the movies, which, stacked one on top of the other in the trunk, crushed my poor flexible black travel bag and the three impeccably ironed shirts it contained. I'd kept a low profile as the equipment was being loaded, I know it's not a good idea to show too much of an interest when heavy lifting is being done (before you know it, you're doing the work yourself), so I'd discreetly moved away across the parking lot while chewing on a matchstick, my hands in my pockets, my eyes on the sumptuous hotel pool that could be made out behind the tinted glass of the reception area. Then, as the four of us headed off once more towards Sfax in the comfortable French Institute car, I could see that despite the anxieties clearly visible on her face, the elder of the two women, who was having a hard time getting back her breath and wildly fanning her chest with her hand, had lost none of her good manners and erudition, because, once she'd got over the initial stress which had left her panting breathlessly beside the driver (of course I'd gallantly ceded her the death seat), she turned to me amiably and apologized for having obliged me to take this detour through Sousse. Don't mention it, my dear woman, I said. As I too happen to be quite well mannered (though not very knowledgeable on the subject of piston rods, into whose mysteries she tried in vain to initiate me), the atmosphere soon became very refined and worldly in the French Institute's car, and we exchanged diverse considerations on our respective activities. I asked them about the reasons for their trip, if not about the circumstances of their breakdown, and learned that, apart from the unfortunate setback of having to spend the night in Sousse and leaving their car in the hands of not particularly scrupulous mechanics who'd tried to take them for a long ride while towing their car (a big mistake, they knew the whole region like it was their own dig), it was above all the bleak prospect of spending three weeks in Sfax without a car that worried them the most. All of their hopes now rested on our chauffeur, who'd already had the chance to help them out a couple of years earlier after another breakdown in the same sector (other times, other piston rods) by driving them each morning and evening to their dig and back.

The driver, who remained quiet, depressed perhaps by the bleak prospect under discussion, which seemed to have come crashing down on him in all its gloom, asked us after a while if we'd like to stop to have a drink and stretch our legs and, after talking it over in the back of the car, the two women and I, we answered that no, there was no need, whereupon he slowed down and pulled up in front of a roadside café. Here it is, he said. He got out of the car and, leading me informally by the arm, brought me inside and asked what I'd like to drink (the women were apparently not thirsty). A tea, I said. He gave our order to the owner in Arabic. The café was very dark, deserted, there was a certain freshness in the air compared with the burning noonday heat of the road. I drank my tea, a very hot, extremely sugary mint tea. I wondered if I should pay and, unsure, decided not to, wandering absently away from the counter and taking a few steps further into the darkness of the room. An old faded poster showing a soccer team wearing red and green uniforms was tacked to one wall, a couple of trophies that weren't exactly won yesterday were displayed on a shelf together with a pennant and a few other odds and ends. Slowly I headed over to a blind door marked "toilets" in Roman letters and gave it a discreet push, in vain, it was locked. I left the café, not a sound on the street. The air was burning outside, almost shimmering. I went and took a piss against a wall behind the building then came back out front. From time to time an old tarp-covered car barreled along the highway at top speed, blowing up a cloud of dust as it passed. Here and there in the noonday heat you could catch a glimpse into the cool and welcoming shadows behind the curtains of a few stores lining the road, a bakery, a butcher's, two or three of those typical little North African grocery stores offering nothing but an enigmatic array of large tins of chickpeas or quince jam, a few bottles of soft drinks in a plastic crate on the floor, and, abandoned near the door, a big burlap sack full of who knows what type of seed. I walked a couple of paces on the sidewalk beside the stores, took a kick at a tin can. Further off, near the car, I could see the silhouettes of my two archaeologists waiting for the driver to return. The eldest was sitting on the back seat, the door wide open, and her colleague was standing beside her, almost in profile, with one elbow on the roof as if she were posing for the cover of a sixties fashion magazine. As I came up to them I saw they were absorbed in the French newspaper I'd bought in Tunis which they seemed to be reading with great interest, the elder holding the newspaper wide open on her lap and the other leaning over from time to time and casually pushing back a strand of hair, while the first, determined, dynamic and undaunted, continued to read the sports page of the newspaper aloud with one hand on her glasses, interrupting her reading occasionally to signal her disbelief to her colleague before closing the paper and sitting motionless for a moment, pensive and distressed, her eyes staring into space and slowly filling with tears, because they had just heard—the news hadn't reached them yet in Sousse—of the death of Ayrton Senna two days earlier at the San Marino Grand Prix.

We'd set off once more for Sfax in the French Institute's car and, sitting in the back, I remained silent and was careful each time I moved my feet not to touch the fine green canvas espadrilles of the woman sitting next to me. She was in the middle of explaining to me courteously that it wouldn't be long before we approached the El Djem Coliseum, without doubt one of the most interesting Roman curiosities in the region, which she would make sure to point out to me when we passed it. The driver kept quiet at the wheel and we continued speeding down the long tree-lined straightaway, keeping our eyes peeled for the El Djem Coliseum. I'd heard about the El Djem Coliseum at a dinner the previous evening and I don't know why, for some bizarre reason I'd associated the word with a natural phenomenon, a gorge or an erg, something like the Roccapina Lion or Thermopylae Pass. Needless to say we weren't exactly keeping our eyes peeled for the same thing, the two of us, leaning side by side out the open backseat window, while from time to time I pushed back her long black hair which was flying in the wind and brushing against my face, keeping it out of my eyes and casually detaching a few twisted strands which the wind had blown against my lips. There it is! she cried at last, pointing out the distant silhouette of a small amphitheatre. The El Djem Coliseum, because that's what it was, was in fact a Roman amphitheatre, plain and simple, all it took was a quick look for me to recognize the word and mentally re-associate it with its appropriate image, a Roman amphitheatre in ruins surrounded by fields, tiny on the horizon, its crown abandoned in the emptiness and worn away with time, toward which we advanced in silence, still a good distance from the site—a couple of miles I'd say—and never getting any closer, either, as the road curved around to avoid it.

When we got to Sfax I said good-bye to my archaeologists and went to open the trunk and fish out the remains of my flexible black travel bag from under the heap of archaeological material they'd piled on top. Holding my bag which was still flexible but now somewhat battered, I crossed the street giving them a polite little wave as the car pulled off, then went into the Abou Nawas Hotel where a room had been booked for me. That very evening, changed and refreshed, I gave my reading at the French Institute in Sfax, introduced and questioned by a renowned Sfaxian academic who was the spitting image of my university friend Romano Pistoletto (Ciccio). This Sfaxian academic and myself were sitting side by side at the head table of a conference room in the French Institute, a makeshift arrangement consisting of a long pale green Formica cafeteria table embellished with a complicated network of electric wires and microphones, next to which two mustard glasses and a large bottle of mineral water had been placed for the speakers. Sitting in light-colored wooden classroom chairs, the audience across from us consisted of around eight or nine people (maybe ten with the organizer)—which is to say that the group was very sparse and most of the rows of chairs put out for the audience remained unoccupied. The director of the French Institute, who was biting his lips at the door on the lookout for hypothetical latecomers, finally decided to open the meeting and, advancing to the podium to welcome the audience and present the speakers, turned the floor without further ado over to my distinguished partner, who, his voice stricken with stage fright, gathered his notes and launched into a detailed study of the themes of my books, which he started to analyze one by one in the chronological order of their appearance. The whole time he spoke, in a clear voice that gradually gained assurance, he fingered his bundle of notes with trembling fingers while, sitting next to him at the head table in a totally creased white shirt which I'd only recently rescued from my travel bag, I listened to him with a serious and concentrated look, my long immobile hands crossed on the table, my eyes traveling alternately from his undeniably Pistolettian face to some particularly attentive (or just strikingly female) member of the audience, resting for a moment on the bottle of mineral water in front of us on the table, which was also quite tempting, I must admit, and which I finally ended up opening noiselessly with the bottle opener put there for the speakers, pouring myself a large glass of mineral water without altogether managing to avoid drowning out the speaker's voice for a few moments with a fizzy bubbling of liquid. Without losing the thread of his analyses, Ciccio's look-alike glanced once or twice out of the corner of his eye to see what on earth I was doing. Among the silent and increasingly sleepy group in front of us (who, it must be said, watched me fill my glass with a fleeting burst of goodhearted curiosity), I of course couldn't fail to notice the discreet presence of my two archaeologists, who'd changed and put on a touch of eye shadow, seated six rows back, attentive and studious, a little worried, it seemed to me, preoccupied, as they listened to Ciccio presenting on the subject of, let's face it, my really rather wonderful books.

return to kyoto

The tears didn't come, although I would have welcomed the voluptuous sensation of crying. I was leaning on the rail of Sanjo Bridge, my chest empty, my immobile fingers trembling slightly (I'd drunk too much the night before), looking down at the silently flowing waters of the Kamo. The weather was bleak and gray and I'd pulled my black wool hat down over my ears. People walked behind me on the pedestrian section of the bridge, crossing paths under transparent umbrellas, under blue umbrellas, under beige umbrellas. I'd stopped beside a pillar out of which rose a decorative cast-iron flame and, motionless under the cold rain whose inconveniences I made no attempt to avoid, seeking them out even, turning my face skywards to feel the raindrops splatter against my cheeks, I thought of the time that had passed, and would have liked to add these rainy tears to its flow. At a loss as to what to do with this very pure moment of melancholy, I wondered how to conserve its essence. I was aware of its exceptional nature, of the unique combination of circumstances that had given rise to it (I'd returned to Kyoto exactly a day ago after a two-year absence). Turning my head towards the Sanjo intersection I saw the hills of Kyoto in the distance, which could just be made out in the mist and, marshalling my forces, closing my eyes to concentrate, I tried to let myself be overcome by tears. I knew I probably wouldn't be able to cry, but even if no tears came out, my spirit was weeping. I looked down at the flowing waters of the Kamo, I was standing on the Sanjo bridge, a fixed stare on my face, my spirit in tears. My chest swelling slowly in time with my breathing, I was taken by a warm and sensual wave of melancholy that I did nothing to restrain, letting these few timeless tears flow before me into the Kamo.

Walking on, I crossed the bridge while my eyes lingered on the water behind me. It looked gray and dirty, sluggish and rippled, weary of swirling languidly downstream before flowing over a natural dam in the riverbed. Coming to the crossing, I walked by the entrance to the Keihan subway line and headed toward the streetcar station on the other side of the street. The station gates were locked and, stopping a moment, I put my hands on the bars and saw that the station was silent and empty, apparently abandoned for several weeks. The platforms were deserted, above them rose immense canopies whose pillars were starting to rust. A few advertisements with faded colors, very pale fuchsias and pinks, with incomprehensible, practically obliterated kanji remained pasted on billboards for the benefit of implausible commuters. Crude lattice fences had been put up on either side of the main entrance, into which planks had been nailed in a cross to board up the entryway. The rails had disappeared from the tracks below, making way for a sort of no-man's-land between the platforms, a sprawling gravel landscape strewn with stones and old lighters, broken glass and clumps of weeds that had grown up here and there beside the puddles. I didn't move, there on the other side of the bars, my eyes fixed on those large motionless puddles reflecting the sky, studded relentlessly by the steady drizzle.

This wasn't the first time I'd seen a place I'd frequented in the past disappear in this way, the transformation of a location I'd known, but seeing this desolate spectacle, this abandoned station out of bounds behind iron bars, this deserted station with its disused platforms, whose tracks had become a craggy rain-soaked wasteland and whose main hall with its ticketing machines was now a junkyard where a rickety turnstile lay askew in the mud, I realized that time had passed since I'd left Kyoto. And if this affected me so deeply on that day, it was not only because my senses, numbed by the prevailing grayness and the alcohol in my blood, naturally put me in a melancholic frame of mind, it was also because I suddenly felt sad and powerless at this brusque testimony to the passage of time. It was hardly the result of conscious reasoning, but rather the concrete and painful, fleeting and physical feeling that I myself was part and parcel of time and its passing. Until then, the feeling of being carried along by time had always been attenuated by the fact that I wrote—until then, in a way, writing had been a means of resisting the current that bore me along, a way of inscribing myself in time, of setting landmarks in the immateriality of its flow, incisions, scratches.

JEAN-PHILIPPE TOUSSAINT is the author of nine novels. His writing has been compared to the work of Samuel Beckett, Jacques Tati, and Jim Jarmusch.

A native of Vancouver, JOHN LAMBERT studied philosophy in Paris before moving to Berlin, where he lives with his wife and two children. He has also translated Jean-Philippe Toussaint's second novel *Monsieur*.

FOR A FULL LIST OF PUBLICATIONS, VISIT:
www.dalkeyarchive.com

SELECTED DALKEY ARCHIVE PAPERBACKS

JANICE GALLOWAY, *Foreign Parts.*
  The Trick Is to Keep Breathing.
WILLIAM H. GASS, *Cartesian Sonata and Other Novellas.*
  Finding a Form.
  A Temple of Texts.
  The Tunnel.
  Willie Masters' Lonesome Wife.
GÉRARD GAVARRY, *Hoppla! 1 2 3.*
ETIENNE GILSON,
  The Arts of the Beautiful.
  Forms and Substances in the Arts.
C. S. GISCOMBE, *Giscome Road.*
  Here.
  Prairie Style.
DOUGLAS GLOVER, *Bad News of the Heart.*
  The Enamoured Knight.
WITOLD GOMBROWICZ,
  A Kind of Testament.
KAREN ELIZABETH GORDON, *The Red Shoes.*
GEORGI GOSPODINOV, *Natural Novel.*
JUAN GOYTISOLO, *Count Julian.*
  Juan the Landless.
  Makbara.
  Marks of Identity.
PATRICK GRAINVILLE, *The Cave of Heaven.*
HENRY GREEN, *Back.*
  Blindness.
  Concluding.
  Doting.
  Nothing.
JIŘÍ GRUŠA, *The Questionnaire.*
GABRIEL GUDDING,
  Rhode Island Notebook.
MELA HARTWIG, *Am I a Redundant Human Being?*
JOHN HAWKES, *The Passion Artist.*
  Whistlejacket.
ALEKSANDAR HEMON, ED.,
  Best European Fiction 2010.
AIDAN HIGGINS, *A Bestiary.*
  Balcony of Europe.
  Bornholm Night-Ferry.
  Darkling Plain: Texts for the Air.
  Flotsam and Jetsam.
  Langrishe, Go Down.
  Scenes from a Receding Past.
  Windy Arbours.
ALDOUS HUXLEY, *Antic Hay.*
  Crome Yellow.
  Point Counter Point.
  Those Barren Leaves.
  Time Must Have a Stop.
MIKHAIL IOSSEL AND JEFF PARKER, EDS.,
  Amerika: Russian Writers View the United States.
GERT JONKE, *The Distant Sound.*
  Geometric Regional Novel.
  Homage to Czerny.
  The System of Vienna.
JACQUES JOUET, *Mountain R.*
  Savage.
CHARLES JULIET, *Conversations with Samuel Beckett and Bram van Velde.*
MIEKO KANAI, *The Word Book.*

HUGH KENNER, *The Counterfeiters.*
  Flaubert, Joyce and Beckett: The Stoic Comedians.
  Joyce's Voices.
DANILO KIŠ, *Garden, Ashes.*
  A Tomb for Boris Davidovich.
ANITA KONKKA, *A Fool's Paradise.*
GEORGE KONRÁD, *The City Builder.*
TADEUSZ KONWICKI, *A Minor Apocalypse.*
  The Polish Complex.
MENIS KOUMANDAREAS, *Koula.*
ELAINE KRAF, *The Princess of 72nd Street.*
JIM KRUSOE, *Iceland.*
EWA KURYLUK, *Century 21.*
ERIC LAURRENT, *Do Not Touch.*
VIOLETTE LEDUC, *La Bâtarde.*
SUZANNE JILL LEVINE, *The Subversive Scribe: Translating Latin American Fiction.*
DEBORAH LEVY, *Billy and Girl.*
  Pillow Talk in Europe and Other Places.
JOSÉ LEZAMA LIMA, *Paradiso.*
ROSA LIKSOM, *Dark Paradise.*
OSMAN LINS, *Avalovara.*
  The Queen of the Prisons of Greece.
ALF MAC LOCHLAINN,
  The Corpus in the Library.
  Out of Focus.
RON LOEWINSOHN, *Magnetic Field(s).*
BRIAN LYNCH, *The Winner of Sorrow.*
D. KEITH MANO, *Take Five.*
MICHELINE AHARONIAN MARCOM,
  The Mirror in the Well.
BEN MARCUS,
  The Age of Wire and String.
WALLACE MARKFIELD,
  Teitlebaum's Window.
  To an Early Grave.
DAVID MARKSON, *Reader's Block.*
  Springer's Progress.
  Wittgenstein's Mistress.
CAROLE MASO, *AVA.*
LADISLAV MATEJKA AND KRYSTYNA POMORSKA, EDS.,
  Readings in Russian Poetics: Formalist and Structuralist Views.
HARRY MATHEWS,
  The Case of the Persevering Maltese: Collected Essays.
  Cigarettes.
  The Conversions.
  The Human Country: New and Collected Stories.
  The Journalist.
  My Life in CIA.
  Singular Pleasures.
  The Sinking of the Odradek Stadium.
  Tlooth.
  20 Lines a Day.
ROBERT L. MCLAUGHLIN, ED.,
  Innovations: An Anthology of Modern & Contemporary Fiction.
HERMAN MELVILLE, *The Confidence-Man.*
AMANDA MICHALOPOULOU, *I'd Like.*

FOR A FULL LIST OF PUBLICATIONS, VISIT:
www.dalkeyarchive.com

⊟

SELECTED DALKEY ARCHIVE PAPERBACKS

STEVEN MILLHAUSER,
The Barnum Museum.
In the Penny Arcade.
RALPH J. MILLS, JR.,
Essays on Poetry.
MOMUS, *The Book of Jokes.*
CHRISTINE MONTALBETTI, *Western.*
OLIVE MOORE, *Spleen.*
NICHOLAS MOSLEY, *Accident.*
Assassins.
Catastrophe Practice.
Children of Darkness and Light.
Experience and Religion.
God's Hazard.
The Hesperides Tree.
Hopeful Monsters.
Imago Bird.
Impossible Object.
Inventing God.
Judith.
Look at the Dark.
Natalie Natalia.
Paradoxes of Peace.
Serpent.
Time at War.
The Uses of Slime Mould:
Essays of Four Decades.
WARREN MOTTE,
Fables of the Novel: French Fiction
since 1990.
Fiction Now: The French Novel in
the 21st Century.
Oulipo: A Primer of Potential
Literature.
YVES NAVARRE, *Our Share of Time.*
Sweet Tooth.
DOROTHY NELSON, *In Night's City.*
Tar and Feathers.
ESHKOL NEVO, *Homesick.*
WILFRIDO D. NOLLEDO,
But for the Lovers.
FLANN O'BRIEN,
At Swim-Two-Birds.
At War.
The Best of Myles.
The Dalkey Archive.
Further Cuttings.
The Hard Life.
The Poor Mouth.
The Third Policeman.
CLAUDE OLLIER, *The Mise-en-Scène.*
PATRIK OUŘEDNÍK, *Europeana.*
FERNANDO DEL PASO,
News from the Empire.
Palinuro of Mexico.
ROBERT PINGET, *The Inquisitory.*
Mahu or The Material.
Trio.
MANUEL PUIG,
Betrayed by Rita Hayworth.
The Buenos Aires Affair.
Heartbreak Tango.
RAYMOND QUENEAU, *The Last Days.*
Odile.
Pierrot Mon Ami.
Saint Glinglin.

ANN QUIN, *Berg.*
Passages.
Three.
Tripticks.
ISHMAEL REED,
The Free-Lance Pallbearers.
The Last Days of Louisiana Red.
Ishmael Reed: The Plays.
Reckless Eyeballing.
The Terrible Threes.
The Terrible Twos.
Yellow Back Radio Broke-Down.
JEAN RICARDOU, *Place Names.*
RAINER MARIA RILKE,
The Notebooks of Malte Laurids
Brigge.
JULIÁN RÍOS, *Larva: A Midsummer*
Night's Babel.
Poundemonium.
AUGUSTO ROA BASTOS, *I the Supreme.*
OLIVIER ROLIN, *Hotel Crystal.*
ALIX CLEO ROUBAUD, *Alix's Journal.*
JACQUES ROUBAUD, *The Form of a*
City Changes Faster, Alas, Than
the Human Heart.
The Great Fire of London.
Hortense in Exile.
Hortense Is Abducted.
The Loop.
The Plurality of Worlds of Lewis.
The Princess Hoppy.
Some Thing Black.
LEON S. ROUDIEZ,
French Fiction Revisited.
VEDRANA RUDAN, *Night.*
STIG SÆTERBAKKEN, *Siamese.*
LYDIE SALVAYRE, *The Company of Ghosts.*
Everyday Life.
The Lecture.
Portrait of the Writer as a
Domesticated Animal.
The Power of Flies.
LUIS RAFAEL SÁNCHEZ,
Macho Camacho's Beat.
SEVERO SARDUY, *Cobra* & *Maitreya.*
NATHALIE SARRAUTE,
Do You Hear Them?
Martereau.
The Planetarium.
ARNO SCHMIDT, *Collected Stories.*
Nobodaddy's Children.
CHRISTINE SCHUTT, *Nightwork.*
GAIL SCOTT, *My Paris.*
DAMION SEARLS, *What We Were Doing*
and Where We Were Going.
JUNE AKERS SEESE,
Is This What Other Women Feel Too?
What Waiting Really Means.
BERNARD SHARE, *Inish.*
Transit.
AURELIE SHEEHAN,
Jack Kerouac Is Pregnant.
VIKTOR SHKLOVSKY, *Knight's Move.*
A Sentimental Journey:
Memoirs 1917–1922.
Energy of Delusion: A Book on Plot.

FOR A FULL LIST OF PUBLICATIONS, VISIT:
www.dalkeyarchive.com

Literature and Cinematography.
Theory of Prose.
Third Factory.
Zoo, or Letters Not about Love.
CLAUDE SIMON, *The Invitation.*
PIERRE SINIAC, *The Collaborators.*
JOSEF ŠKVORECKÝ, *The Engineer of Human Souls.*
GILBERT SORRENTINO,
  Aberration of Starlight.
  Blue Pastoral.
  Crystal Vision.
  Imaginative Qualities of Actual Things.
  Mulligan Stew.
  Pack of Lies.
  Red the Fiend.
  The Sky Changes.
  Something Said.
  Splendide-Hôtel.
  Steelwork.
  Under the Shadow.
W. M. SPACKMAN,
  The Complete Fiction.
ANDRZEJ STASIUK, *Fado.*
GERTRUDE STEIN,
  Lucy Church Amiably.
  The Making of Americans.
  A Novel of Thank You.
LARS SVENDSEN, *A Philosophy of Evil.*
PIOTR SZEWC, *Annihilation.*
GONÇALO M. TAVARES, *Jerusalem.*
LUCIAN DAN TEODOROVICI,
  Our Circus Presents . . .
STEFAN THEMERSON, *Hobson's Island.*
  The Mystery of the Sardine.
  Tom Harris.
JEAN-PHILIPPE TOUSSAINT,
  The Bathroom.
  Camera.
  Monsieur.
  Running Away.
  Self-Portrait Abroad.
  Television.
DUMITRU TSEPENEAG,
  The Necessary Marriage.
  Pigeon Post.
  Vain Art of the Fugue.
ESTHER TUSQUETS, *Stranded.*
DUBRAVKA UGRESIC,
  Lend Me Your Character.
  Thank You for Not Reading.
MATI UNT, *Brecht at Night*
  Diary of a Blood Donor.
  Things in the Night.
ÁLVARO URIBE AND OLIVIA SEARS, EDS.,
  Best of Contemporary Mexican Fiction.
ELOY URROZ, *The Obstacles.*
LUISA VALENZUELA, *He Who Searches.*
MARJA-LIISA VARTIO,
  The Parson's Widow.
PAUL VERHAEGHEN, *Omega Minor.*
BORIS VIAN, *Heartsnatcher.*
ORNELA VORPSI, *The Country Where No One Ever Dies.*
AUSTRYN WAINHOUSE, *Hedyphagetica.*

PAUL WEST,
  Words for a Deaf Daughter & *Gala.*
CURTIS WHITE,
  America's Magic Mountain.
  The Idea of Home.
  Memories of My Father Watching TV.
  Monstrous Possibility: An Invitation to Literary Politics.
  Requiem.
DIANE WILLIAMS, *Excitability: Selected Stories.*
  Romancer Erector.
DOUGLAS WOOLF, *Wall to Wall.*
  Ya! & *John-Juan.*
JAY WRIGHT, *Polynomials and Pollen.*
  The Presentable Art of Reading Absence.
PHILIP WYLIE, *Generation of Vipers.*
MARGUERITE YOUNG,
  Angel in the Forest.
  Miss MacIntosh, My Darling.
REYOUNG, *Unbabbling.*
ZORAN ŽIVKOVIĆ, *Hidden Camera.*
LOUIS ZUKOFSKY, *Collected Fiction.*
SCOTT ZWIREN, *God Head.*